D0332620

For Doreen … clear head and loyal
supporter of … tures!

FIFE COUNCIL
CENTRAL AREA

801466		
PETERS	23-Oct-07	
JF	£5.99	
JSAS	RH	

Red Robin BOOKS
Where story matters

Red Robin Books is an imprint of Corner To Learn Limited

Published by

Corner To Learn Limited
Willow Cottage • 26 Purton Stoke
Swindon • Wiltshire SN5 4JF • UK

ISBN 978-1-905434-12-1

First published in the UK 2007
Text © Neil Griffiths 2007
Illustrations © Peggy Collins 2007

The rights of Neil Griffiths to be identified as the
author of this work has been asserted by him in accordance
with the Copyright, Designs and Patents Act 1988.

All rights reserved.
No part of this publication may be reproduced, stored in a
retrieval system, or transmitted in any form or by any means,
electronic, mechanical, photocopying, recording, or otherwise,
without the prior written permission of the Publisher. Any person
who does any unauthorised act in relation to this publication may
be liable to criminal prosecution and civil claims for damages.

Design by
David Rose

Printed by
Tien Wah Press Pte. Ltd.,
Singapore

Tallula's Atishoo!

Neil Griffiths

Illustrated by **Peggy Collins**

Tallula was doing what she liked to do most of all, wallowing in mud! She loved the stuff. The stickier the better! In fact, given the chance, she would sit in it all day long, and today she was doing just that. How happy she was!

The sun warmed her back and mud oozed between her toes. "Lovely," she thought, "just lovely!"

By lunchtime, the sun had become a little too hot and began to toast the tiny hairs on her back, so she sank deeper into the cool slimy mud.

By tea-time, she had sunk so much that all you could see were her two round eyes and huge nostrils, peering from the muddy surface.

As night began to fall, she felt the air begin to chill and decided it was time for bed in the warmth of the reeds. She tried to lift her feet, but they wouldn't move. She tried again, but they were stuck firmly in the oozing mud. She'd been in it for too long and had sunk into the murky depths.

"Help," cried Tallula. "Help, I'm stuck," she wailed. Her cries were heard deep in the jungle and Edith, Gerald, Zandra, Livingstone, Hartley, Baldwin, Priscilla and Maxwell rushed to the mud pool to see what all the commotion was about.

"I can't move, I'm stuck. Please get me out, it's so cold," pleaded a shivering Tallula. "Don't worry, I'll get you out with no trouble," trumpeted Edith.

She curled her long trunk and pulled with all her strength. But Tallula didn't move an inch.

"I need help," called Edith. "Grab hold of my tail, Gerald, and pull as hard as you can!" she ordered.

Gerald did as he was told and pulled and
pulled, but it hurt Edith so much that
she gave out a huge cry
and let go of Tallula.

"We need more help," said Gerald, so Zandra and Livingstone took a firm hold. Gerald held Edith by her large legs this time. "Pull," she commanded. But still Tallula didn't budge and Zandra began to get nervous that Livingstone might get tempted to eat her, so couldn't stop shaking!

This time, Hartley, Baldwin and Priscilla joined the line and took hold. But just as they began to pull, one of Priscilla's spines stuck in Baldwin's bottom, he let out a yell, Hartley burst into hysterical laughter and everyone fell down!

Priscilla promised to keep her spines in and Maxwell grabbed hold for one last effort.

"Right," said Edith. "Now give it all you've got!" she bellowed. They pulled and pulled and pulled! But Tallula remained as stuck as she ever had been.

"Help!" whimpered Tallula. "It's getting colder," she shivered.

"I'll get her out," said a tiny voice.

"Who's that?" they all asked.

"Me," said a tiny fly.

"You?" they all laughed and wailed.

"Yes me," said the fly confidently.

"But how will a tiny fly like you get Tallula out, when we have all tried?" chuckled Edith.

"Just watch," said fly. "But I'd take cover if I were you," he warned.

"Take cover, my trunk!" snorted Edith. "As if he'll be any help," she sneered.

The fly flew straight up one of Tallula's nostrils
as the other animals looked on curiously.
Tallula began to shudder and the ground began to
shake and she suddenly let out the biggest...

Aaatishoooo...!

In fact, it was so powerful that it blew her and all the mud out of the pond.

Tallula shook herself, thanked the fly and plodded off.
"It was nothing," he replied, smiling proudly at the other animals, all of whom were wishing they had listened to his warning!